Janyra's First Day

by Shika Gaines

illustrated by Amy Koch Johnson

This book is dedicated to my best friend, Janaye and her daughter Jordyn. Jordyn is now in heaven. I know in my heart that Jordyn and Zion (My daughter) will be best friends in heaven one day.

I will also like to dedicate this book to my sweet daughter, Zion Renee Demares.

Dear Zion,
I love you. I wrote this book when you were in my womb.

Janyra is moving from Chicago to Arizona.

She will be attending
Mt. Zion Elementary.

On the first day of school, she meets her teachers and classmates. Her teacher's name is Miss Liwensky.

She walks in her class, and she notices she looks different from the other students. Miss Lewinsky introduces her as Janyra.

The students begin to whisper and laugh at her name. Janyra is instantly uncomfortable and feels self-conscious.

Right before recess one of her classmates walks up and says; "Hi, I'm Stan! Whoa you have a tan. Don't look so frazzled, by the way cool hair and it's badazzled!"

He picks a hand full of her braided beads and drops them against one another. The noise rings through out the hall, click clack click clack.

"Nice meeting you Janaye."

And then Stan runs off.

Janyra is left by herself,
and she thinks these
thoughts:

What's a tan?

Who's Janaye?

My hair is badazzled!

At the end of the day Janyra's Mom picks her up in the car.

"Mom what's a tan?" Janyra asks.

"A tan is when your skin gets darker after baking in the sun. Why do you ask baby?" Mom responds.

"Well, Stan said I had a tan."

Mom smirks, "Well, how was your day? Did you meet any new people?"

"Yes! There's uh, there is Cindy, Beau, Nessa, Lindsey, Ngoc, Joc and Ms. Liwensky!" Exclaimed Janyra.

On the next day of school, Janyra sees one of her classmates.

"Hello, I'm Cindy. How are you Janaye? I must say, you look glowey today. What is that on your face?" Cindy takes her finger and glides it across her face.

Janyra responds, "Cocoa butter." Then she walks off in a fury as her beads go click, clack, click, clack.

Cindy looks confused and whispers, "Cocoa butter?"

On the ride home, Mom asks, "How was your day?"

Janyra burst out in tears, yelling, "It was a day, a day, I have to say! Why didn't you just name me Janaye? Janyra is way to hard to Say! They call me Janaye anyway!" Mom replies, "Calm down young Lady, let's be fair! It's good to be different."

Janyra cuts her mom off and yells, "I don't wanna be fair and I'm sick of this hair... it's way too noisy!"

"So who is mispronouncing your name?" Mama asks.

Janyra responds, "Well, it's Cindy, Beau, Nessa, Lindsey, Ngoc, Joc and even Ms. Liwensky!"

The next day at school, a group of kids call her, "Janaye, Janaye come and play!"

Janyra stomps towards the crowd and her beads are extra loud. Her fists balled up and she blows, yelling out, "I've tried, I've tried with all my might to pronounce all of your names right. Please do your homework and learn mine, it shouldn't take all night, right? If I can do it so can you! There's Cindy, Stan, Beau, Nessa, Lindsey, Ngoc, Joc and Ms. Liwensky! There's one of me and many of you! What's a girl left to do?"

"I understand, Stan thinks I'm tan. I understand, Cindy thinks I'm glowey. But, what I can't understand is, why must you guys think I'm Janaye? My name is Janyra, not Janaye."

Ngoc interjects, "Whoa, whoa, calm down, Janyra is all you had to say. We got it! No more Janaye. And trust me I get it, they called me Nick for months. It bothered me, but I never had the courage to admit it."

All the kids yell at once, "Janyra okay, no more Janaye, we promise! Just please come and play!"

3 Tips To Help You Honor Your Friend's Unique Name

Ja•Ny•Ra

1. Be Honest-
Tell them you are having trouble, and ask them to repeat their name.
2. Be Considerate-
Ask your friend if he or she likes to be called by a nickname until you fully grasp his or her name.
3. Be Dedicated-
You have to truly want to pronounce his or her name correctly. Start by clapping each syllable of his or her name.

For Instance-

Ja 👏 Ny 👏 Ra 👏

Made in the USA
San Bernardino, CA
11 April 2019